"HELLO READING books are a perfect introduction to reading. Brief sentences full of word repetition and full-color pictures stress visual clues to help a child take the first important steps toward reading. Mastering these story books will build children's reading confidence and give them the enthusiasm to stand on their own in the world of words."

—Bee Cullinan
Past President of the International Reading
Association, Professor in New York University's
Early Childhood and Elementary Education Program

"Readers aren't born, they're made. Desire is planted—planted by parents who work at it."

—Jim Trelease
author of *The Read Aloud Handbook*

"When I was a classroom reading teacher, I recognized the importance of good stories in making children understand that reading is more than just recognizing words. I saw that children who have ready access to story books get excited about reading. They also make noticeably greater gains in reading comprehension. The development of the HELLO READING stories grows out of this experience."

—Harriet Ziefert
M.A.T., New York University School of Education
Author, Language Arts Module,
Scholastic Early Childhood Program

For Janet Schulman

PUFFIN BOOKS
Viking Penguin Inc., 40 West 23rd Street, New York, New York 10010, U.S.A.
Penguin Books Ltd, 27 Wrights Lane, London W8 5TZ (Publishing & Editorial) and
Harmondsworth, Middlesex, England (Distribution & Warehouse)
Penguin Books Australia Ltd., Ringwood, Victoria, Australia
Penguin Books Canada Limited, 2801 John St., Markham, Ontario, Canada L3R 1B4
Penguin Books (N.Z.) Ltd, 182–190 Wairau Road, Auckland 10, New Zealand

First published in Puffin Books, 1988 • Published simultaneously in Canada
Text copyright © Harriet Ziefert, 1988
Illustrations copyright © Claire Schumacher, 1988
All rights reserved • Printed in Singapore for Harriet Ziefert, Inc.

Library of Congress Cataloging-in-Publication Data
Ziefert, Harriet.
Cat games / Harriet Ziefert; pictures by Claire Schumacher.
p. cm.—(Hello reading! ; 7)
Summary: Two cats, Matt and Pat, play hide and seek and a chasing game.
ISBN 0-14-050809-0
[1. Cats—Fiction. 2. Hide-and-seek—Fiction. 3. Games—Fiction]
I. Schumacher, Claire, ill. II. Title. III. Series: Ziefert, Harriet.
Hello reading! (Puffin Books) ; 7.
PZ7.Z487Cat 1988b [E]—dc19   87-25805   CIP AC

CAT GAMES

Harriet Ziefert
Pictures by Claire Schumacher

PUFFIN BOOKS

Chapter One
Hide-and-Seek

Where are the cats?

One orange cat
up in a tree.
One gray cat
under a tree.

Up in a tree is Pat.
Under the tree is Matt.
Matt calls.
He wants Pat to come down.

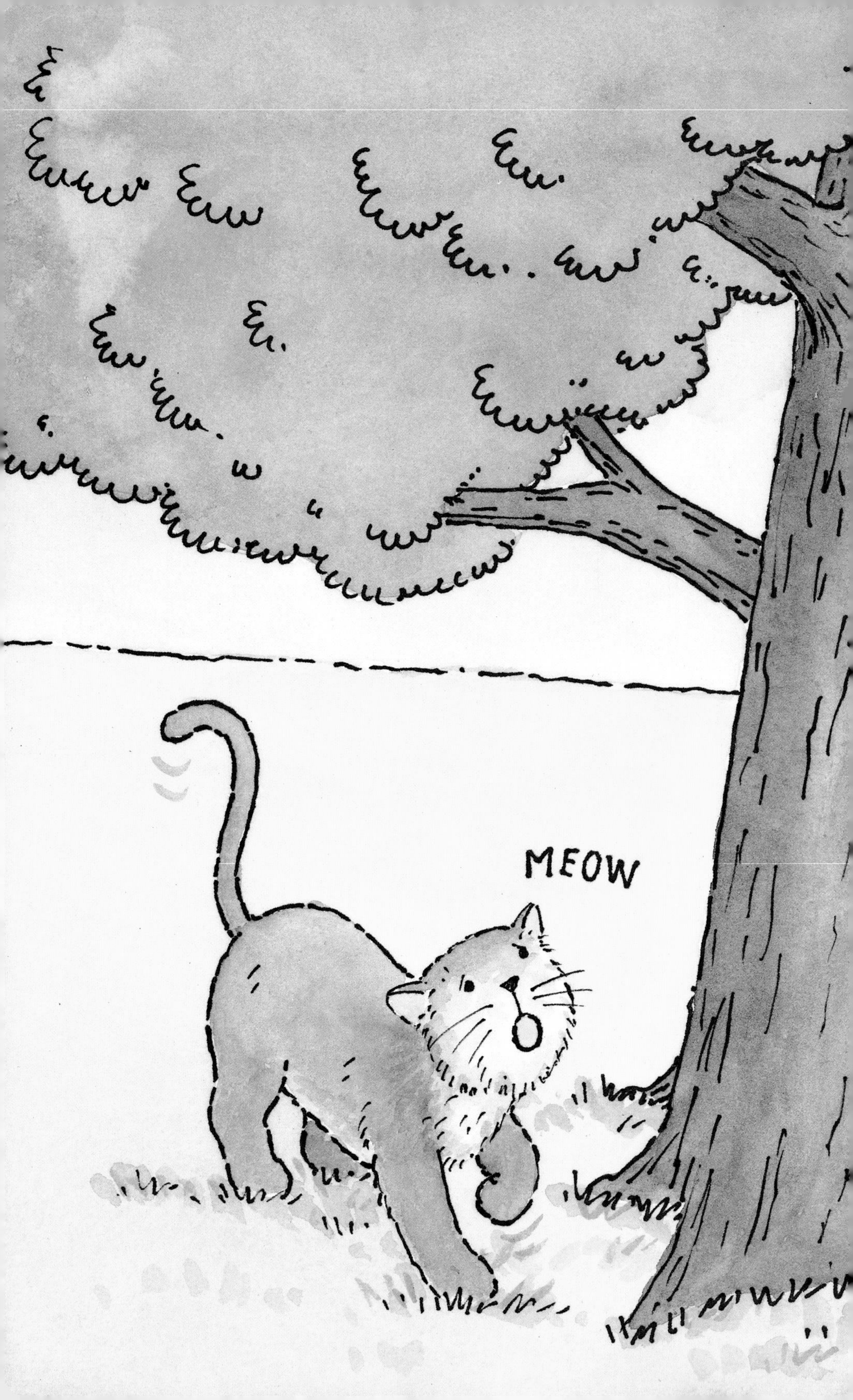
MEOW

Pat looks down at Matt.
Then she jumps higher!

One cat still up in the tree.
One cat still under the tree.
Up in the tree is she.
Under the tree is he.

Matt calls again.
He wants Pat to come down.
But she wants to go higher.

MEOW

Pat jumps again!

Now Matt can't see Pat.
So he climbs up the tree.

Pat hides.

Matt seeks.

Two cats play
hide-and-seek.

Where is she?
Where is he?

Where is the gray cat?
Where is the orange cat?
Can you see them?

Chapter Two
New Game

Two cats play
a new game.

Pat runs.
Matt runs after her.

Matt chases Pat
around and around.

Matt runs.
Pat runs after him.

Pat chases Matt
around and around.

Along comes a barking dog.
He chases Matt and Pat.

Up the tree runs Matt.
Up the tree runs Pat.

Under the tree is
the barking dog.
He wants to play.
The dog looks up
at Pat and Matt.

Pat and Matt look down
at the dog.

Pat looks at Matt.
Matt looks at Pat.

They look up and down.
And then...

they jump!

Two cats
and a dog
play under a tree!